Mikissuk's Secret

Written by Isabelle Lafonta
Illustrated by Barroux

Scholastic Canada Ltd.
Toronto New York London Auckland Sydney
Mexico City New Delhi Hong Kong Buenos Aires

Mikissuk was a happy girl. She loved to laugh, and she was happiest of all when she was with her big brother Sorqaq. He made toys out of caribou horn for her, and when Mikissuk walked out across the ice in his footsteps, nothing could frighten her. With his big hand wrapped firmly around hers, she felt as strong as a polar bear.

But lately, everything had changed.

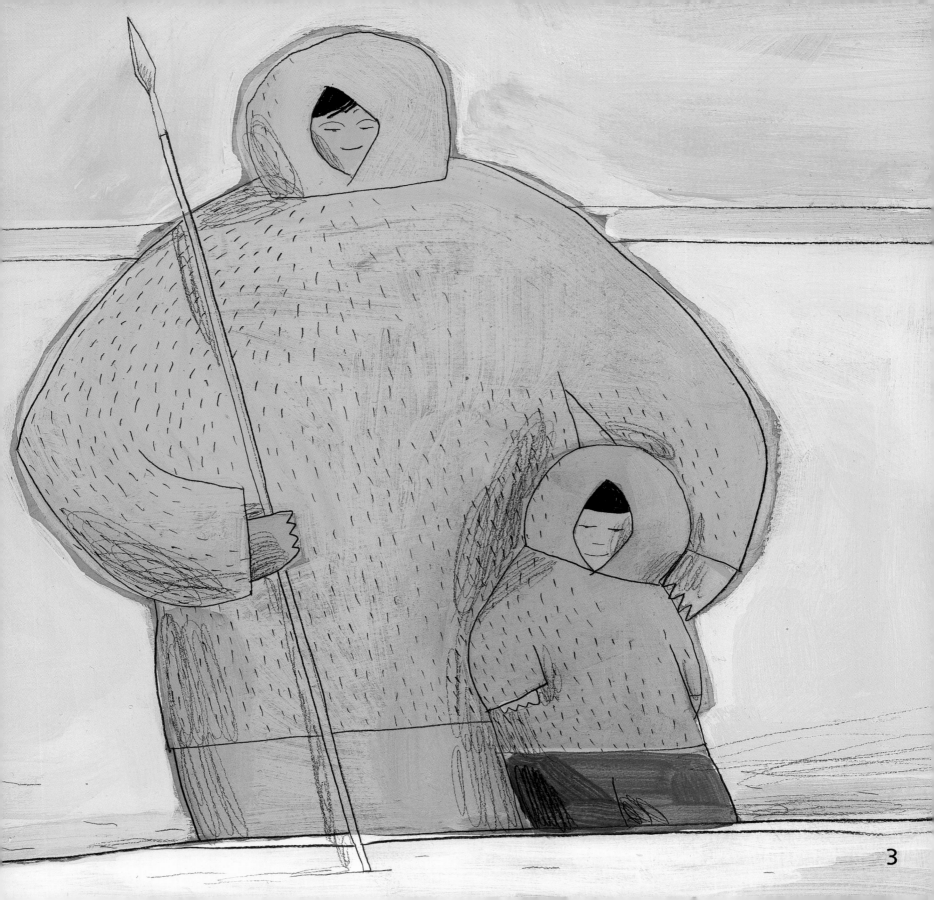

Mikissuk sat all alone at the frosty window of their winter house. She felt as transparent as a drop of melting snow, as if she were invisible to Sorqaq. For weeks he had spent all his time outside, building himself a dogsled.

Every day it grew closer to being finished. Every day, Mikissuk grew angrier. "I might as well not exist!" she grumbled. But nothing distracted Sorqaq from his work.

Mikissuk's secret wish was that her brother would take her hunting with him when the dogsled was finished. Every night she dreamed of flying across the ice on the sled, holding her very own harpoon high above her head.

"Have you thought about a place for me on your sled?" she finally asked Sorqaq, so quietly that he could barely hear her above the crackle of the blazing fire.

Surprised, Sorqaq would not meet her eyes.
"You're too little," he said. "Out on the ice, the wind cuts
sharper than a knife. You have to be a rock to stand up to it.
You're soft and small — more like a flower than a rock!"

That night Mikissuk dreamed that her head could touch the sky. The clouds wrapped around her like scarves, and the blizzard kissed her gently on the cheek.

But when morning came, nothing had changed.
Mikissuk stared at her reflection in the window pane.
"Mikissuk," she said to herself. "The Little One.
That's what I am. Too small."

Sorqaq was already up, rubbing the dogs' harness with whale oil.
Before he set out for his first ride on the new sled, he waved
goodbye: "Just you wait, my little snow-star, I'll bring back
the finest furs in Nunavut for you!"

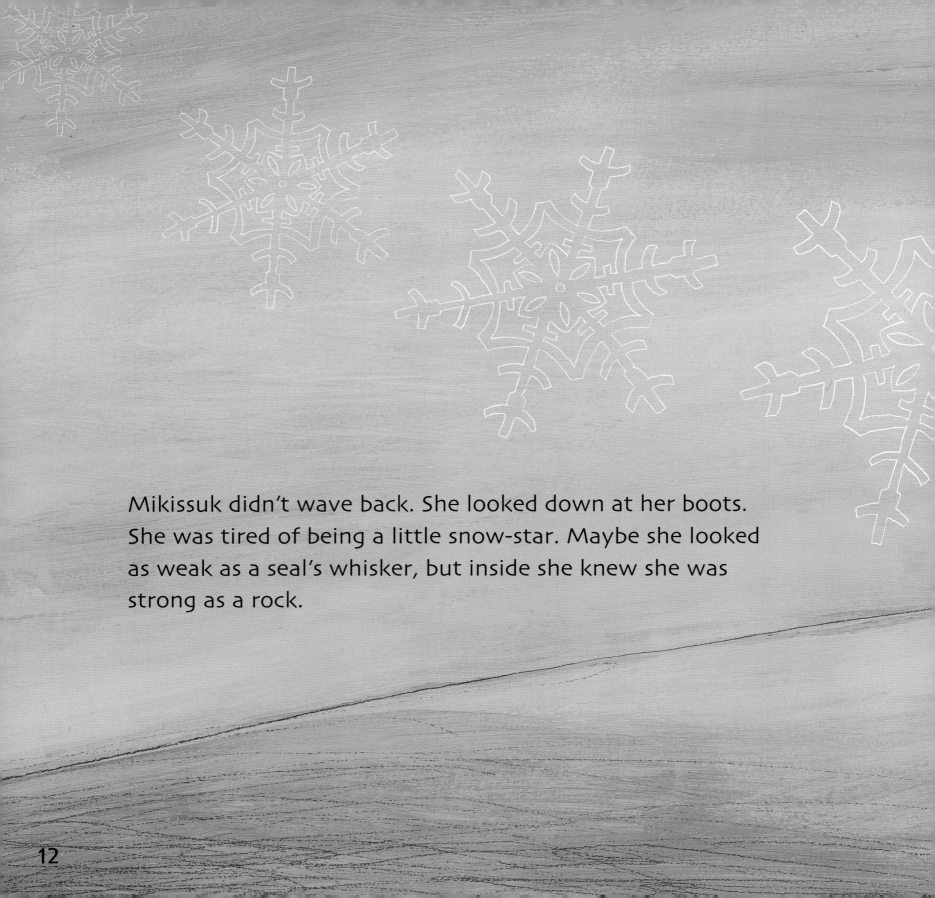

Mikissuk didn't wave back. She looked down at her boots. She was tired of being a little snow-star. Maybe she looked as weak as a seal's whisker, but inside she knew she was strong as a rock.

Why couldn't her brother see that?
"How can I open his eyes?" she sighed.
Then she had an idea.

"Mother, is there a piece of seal tendon I could have? Please?"

"Of course you can. What do you want it for?" her mother asked.
"A belt for your doll?"

"It's a secret," said Mikissuk.

From that moment on, Mikissuk was busy. First she chewed
the tendon to make it soft. Then she stretched and stretched
it to make a long piece of string. Thanks to her secret,
the long, dark winter days flew by as lightly as snowflakes.

16

One morning, a ribbon of light floated above the ice.

"Look, Mikissuk!" said her mother. "Winter is over!"

Mikissuk smiled. Once the pack ice started melting,
Sorqaq would no longer be able to go out hunting on
his sled!

When he got back from his trip, Sorqaq showed off the beautiful furs he had brought home. But Mikissuk was as silent and cold as ice. Sorqaq stomped off and flung down his harpoon.

Mikissuk thought of her secret and quivered with impatience. "Now I need some driftwood," she said. But Sorqaq was the one who would have to get it for her!

"All right," he said. "But you have to do something for me, too. Get me some eggs from the island."

It was a lot of work for one piece of driftwood! Mikissuk had to paddle through fierce currents to get to the island, then climb up the rocks with the wings of the birds fluttering around her. By the time she got home she was exhausted.

"There, Sorqaq! My bag is full to the brim!" she announced. "Now, keep your promise."

The wind blew over the ice cliffs.
It was so cold that Mikissuk felt as if she
was being pinched by thousands of icy fingers.
Still she sat stubbornly outside, shaping the long
branch of driftwood she had won from her brother.

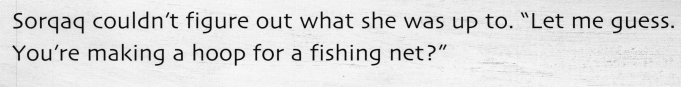

Sorqaq couldn't figure out what she was up to. "Let me guess. You're making a hoop for a fishing net?"

"It's a secret," said Mikissuk.

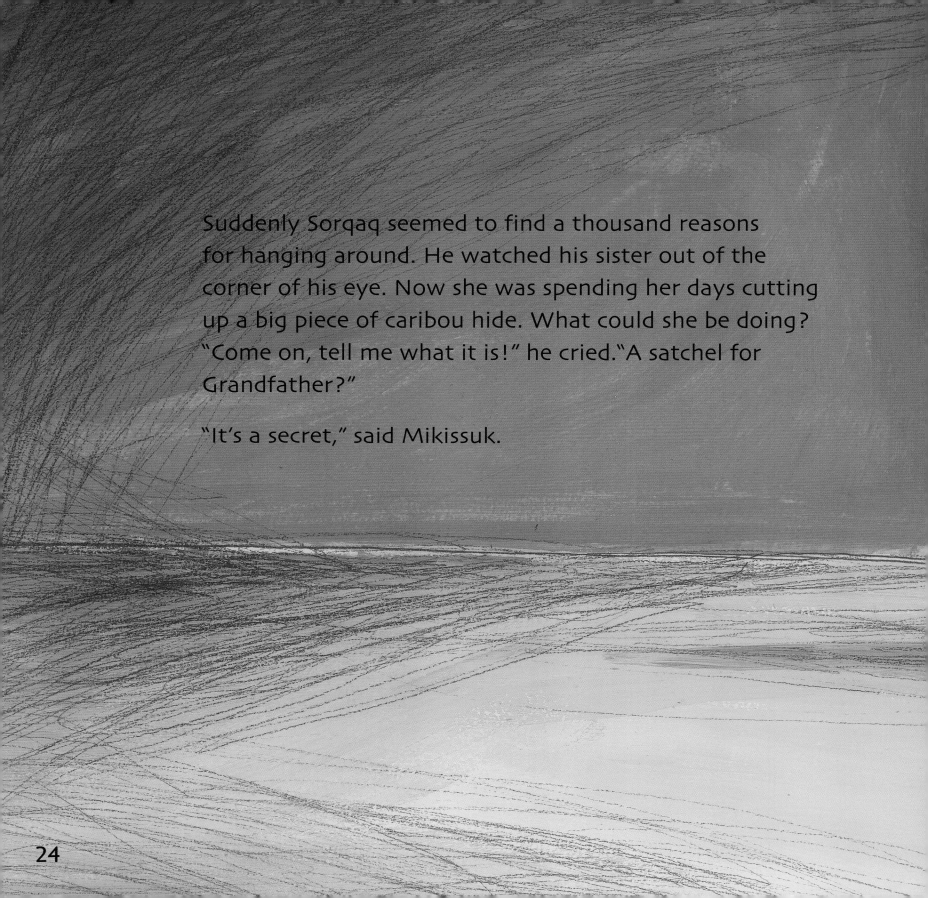

Suddenly Sorqaq seemed to find a thousand reasons for hanging around. He watched his sister out of the corner of his eye. Now she was spending her days cutting up a big piece of caribou hide. What could she be doing? "Come on, tell me what it is!" he cried. "A satchel for Grandfather?"

"It's a secret," said Mikissuk.

24

Now the mystery was all Sorqaq could think about.
Round and round his head it whirled. He even
forgot to go hunting. But of course, the family had
to eat. At last, he harnessed the huskies and set out.

Mikissuk made the most of her brother's absence.
She used the seal tendon to fasten the caribou skin
to the hoop of driftwood. "Thanks to you, my dream
will soon come true," she whispered, hiding her
treasure away.

26

Sorqaq returned from his hunting trip exhausted. His sled felt as heavy as a whale as he put it away. "Maybe it's too big for me after all," he admitted to himself for the first time.

Slowly Mikissuk approached him. "Do you remember what you told me about hunting? You said I would need to be able to face up to the north wind. Well, I'm going to show you that I am not afraid." Her heart thumped as she opened her bag.

She took out the drum that she had spent so much time making, and she began to play. She played so well that with each beat, she seem to grow larger. As strong as a polar bear, the song of the drum rose into the sky, drowning out the howling of the wind.

Sorqaq stared in amazement. Could this be his little sister, stronger than the winter storms, making his heart pound along with her drum?

"I think I've discovered your secret,"
said Sorqaq. "You may be small,
but you have a will of stone."
And he held out a package
to his sister.

Now it was Mikissuk's turn to be amazed. She opened the package and her eyes sparkled like stars. There, lying on a silver sealskin, was a glittering harpoon. It was even more beautiful than she had dreamed.

Under the cold polar skies Mikissuk and Sorqaq smiled at each other as equals. Their laughs rang out, dancing along the trail where, tomorrow, their sled would carry them toward their dreams.

NUNAVUT

Mikissuk lives in Nunavut, Canada's third northern territory, created on April 1, 1999. Its capital city is Iqaluit.

Nunavut is made up of islands and rocky outcrops. For eight to ten months of the year, snow covers the territory. For many weeks, the people of Nunavut live in darkness.

Then, when summer comes, it is light all the time — it's like a two-month-long daytime. Here and there, the midnight sun melts the ice and patches of tundra appear.

The native people of Nunavut are called Inuit, which in their language, Inuktitut, means "human being."

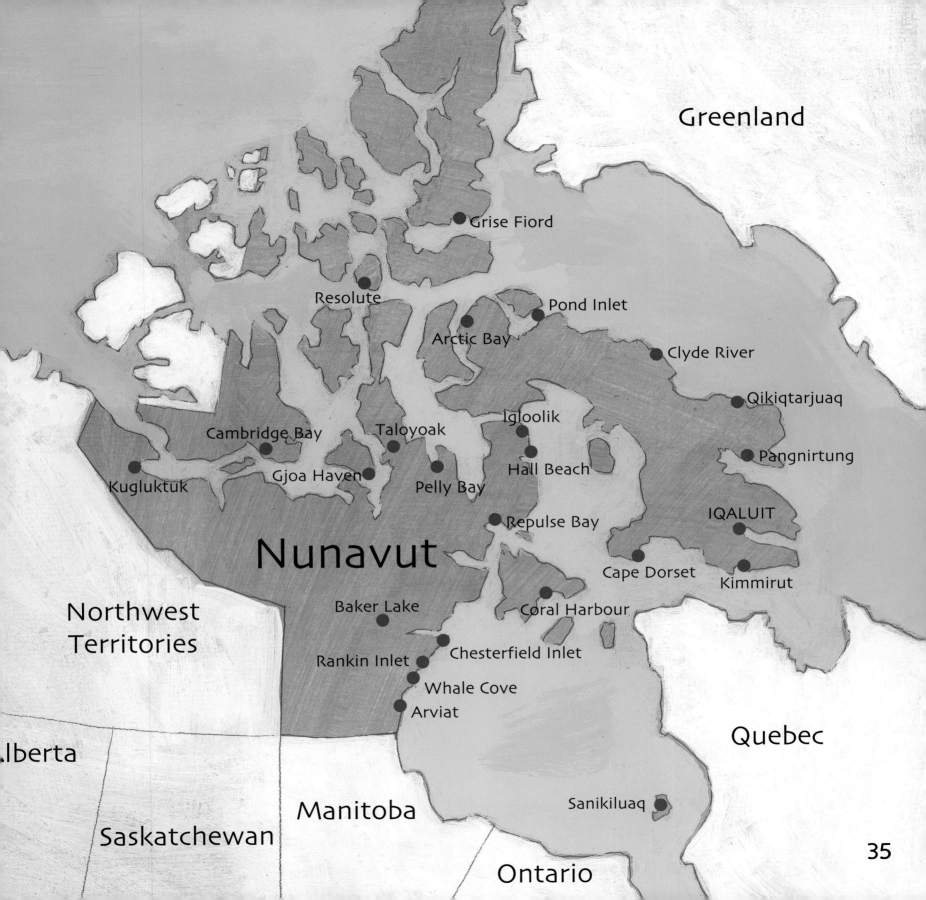

Greenland

Grise Fiord

Resolute

Pond Inlet

Arctic Bay

Clyde River

Qikiqtarjuaq

Cambridge Bay

Taloyoak

Igloolik

Pangnirtung

Kugluktuk

Gjoa Haven

Hall Beach

Pelly Bay

Nunavut

IQALUIT

Repulse Bay

Cape Dorset

Kimmirut

Northwest
Territories

Baker Lake

Coral Harbour

Rankin Inlet

Chesterfield Inlet

Whale Cove

Arviat

Quebec

lberta

Manitoba

Sanikiluaq

Saskatchewan

Ontario

The Creatures of the Far North

The Inuit classify animals by the way they carry themselves, and distinguish between *pisuktiit* (creatures that walk), *tingmiat* (creatures that fly) and *puijiit* (sea mammals), which lift their heads out of the water to breathe.

The polar bear — *nanuq*

A meat eater and an excellent swimmer, the polar bear lives on seals and fish. His meat and pelt are prized by hunters, and his claws, hung on a leather thread, are worn to bring good luck.

The caribou — *tuktu*

Caribou are herbivores, or plant eaters. They live on the tundra and travel thousands of kilometres each year to find new pastures. Their hide is used to make winter clothes and their antlers to make tools.

The ivory gull — *naujavaaq*

A scavenger, the ivory gull lives mainly on the carcasses of mammals left by predators such as polar bears. Gull eggs were considered a great delicacy and feathers were used to make brooms and clothing.

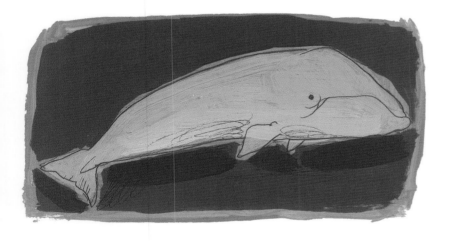

The bowhead whale — *arvitt*

Often seen alone, the bowhead whale swims near to the shore. Whale flesh and fat are favourite foods of the Inuit. In the past, the oil of the bowhead whale was used as fuel for lamps and its bones were used for building.

The bearded seal — *ugyuk*

This seal spends its time in shallow waters and on ice floes. It is valued for its meat as well as its hide, which is used to make waterproof clothing.

Traditional Inuit Clothing

Nowadays, many Inuit wear pullovers and parkas made in factories. But others remain faithful to the clothing designed by their ancestors.

Mittens — *pualuit*

Pualuit are made of sealskin because it is waterproof and very tough. The wrists are often decorated with the fur of polar bears or arctic foxes.

Boots — *kamiit*

Kamiit are made out of bearskin for winter use, and out of sealskin for summer. They are tied at the top with a cord, and are made up of a sole sewn to a leg piece, which is knee-high.

Hooded jacket — *amauti*

Woman wear amauti, a jacket with a big hood, made from seal or caribou skin. The hood enables them to carry their babies and shelter them from the wind at the same time.

The Music of Nunavut

Developed to brighten up the long, dark days of winter,
the musical traditions of Nunavut are playful and festive.
At any gathering, there is lots of singing
and dancing to drums.

The drum — *qilaut*

The qilaut is the symbol of Inuit culture. It is traditionally used to invoke spirits and to communicate with the natural elements to ask them to protect hunters. Nowadays, it is most often used to accompany storytellers and dancers.

Throat singing — *qatajaq*

To entertain their children, Inuit women play games with their voices. Standing opposite each other, they make their throats vibrate in a way that makes a sound like the whistling of the wind or the cries of animals. The first one to laugh or to run out of breath is the loser!

Scholastic Canada Ltd.
604 King Street West, Toronto, Ontario M5V 1E1, Canada

Scholastic Inc.
557 Broadway, New York, NY 10012, USA

Scholastic Australia Pty Limited
PO Box 579, Gosford, NSW 2250, Australia

Scholastic New Zealand Limited
Private Bag 94407, Greenmount, Auckland, New Zealand

Scholastic Children's Books
Euston House, 24 Eversholt Street, London NW1 1DB, UK

To Paul, Fernande and Lucille
and to all who love the faraway countries born out of a tiny seed. — *I.L.*

To Paul-Émile Victor, For Milan and Félix. — *B.*

Library and Archives Canada Cataloguing in Publication

Lafonta, Isabelle
Mikissuk's secret / written by Isabelle Lafonta ; illustrations by Barroux.
Translation of: Le secret de Mikissuk.
ISBN 978-0-545-99610-5
I. Barroux II. Title.

PZ7.L325Mi 2008   j843'.92   C2007-905148-0

ISBN-10 0-545-99610-4

Text by Isabelle Lafonta; illustrations by Barroux.
Copyright © 2006 Hatier, Paris.
All rights reserved.

6 5 4 3 2 1   Printed in Singapore   08 09 10 11 12